EVERY
TIME
A
RAINBOW
DIES

ALSO BY
RITA WILLIAMS-GARCIA

BLUE TIGHTS

CLAYTON BYRD GOES UNDERGROUND

FAST TALK ON A SLOW TRACK

JUMPED

LIKE SISTERS ON THE HOMEFRONT

NO LAUGHTER HERE

A SITTING IN ST. JAMES

THE GAITHER SISTERS TRILOGY

ONE CRAZY SUMMER

P.S. BE ELEVEN

GONE CRAZY IN ALABAMA

EVERY TIME A RAINBOW DIES

RITA WILLIAMS-GARCIA

Quill Tree Books
An Imprint of HarperCollinsPublishers

The author would like to acknowledge
Ann-Marie Young for her assistance with this novel.

Quill Tree Books is an imprint of HarperCollins Publishers.

Every Time a Rainbow Dies
Copyright © 2001 by Rita Williams-Garcia
All rights reserved. Printed in the United States of America.
No part of this book may be used or reproduced in any
manner whatsoever without written permission except in
the case of brief quotations embodied in critical articles and
reviews. For information address HarperCollins Children's
Books, a division of HarperCollins Publishers, 195 Broadway,
New York, NY 10007.
www.epicreads.com

Library of Congress Cataloging-in-Publication Data
Williams-Garcia, Rita.
Every time a rainbow dies / Rita Williams-Garcia.
    p.   cm.
Summary: After seeing a girl raped and becoming obsessed with her,
sixteen-year-old Thulani finds motivation to move beyond his interest in
his pigeons and his grief over his mother's death.
ISBN 978-0-06-307926-7
[1. Caribbean Americans—Fiction. 2. Interpersonal relations—Fiction.
3. Rape—Fiction. 4. Brothers—Fiction. 5. Pigeons—Fiction. 6. New York
(N.Y.)—Fiction. I. Title.
PZ7.W6713 Ev 2001   00-38900
[Fic]—dc21   CIP
                                                                       AC

Typography by Alison Donalty and Catherine San Juan
21 22 23 24 25   PC/LSCH   10 9 8 7 6 5 4 3 2 1
❖
First Quill Tree Books Edition, 2021
Revisions to the original text have been made by the author.

For Michelle Renee and Elizabeth Mark

EVERY
TIME
A
RAINBOW
DIES

ONE

From on top of Brooklyn, Thulani watched the sun bed the clouds, waiting, as he always did, for his birds to return. He woke each morning with one thought: freeing his birds. Their cooing pulled him from sleep, called him up the attic steps and onto the roof of his brownstone. Each and every time it gave him a thrill to unlatch the door of the dovecote he had built and find himself besieged by fourteen pigeons, each a variation of white: snowy, spotted, dingy, or wing-stained. Every morning without fail he dropped cereal or seeds on the asphalt roof, recalled the meanderings of dreams better told to birds than people, then watched them fly off toward Prospect Park. As sure as he knew the view from the rooftop, he knew his birds would always return to him.

Thulani looked out into the graying predusk. Below him, in their apartment, his sister-in-law, Shakira, rubbed her belly, waiting for her husband to come in from work. On the street city buses became scarce, leaving Eastern Parkway to gypsy cabs and vans. Store owners locked up their shops, and street vendors packed up their tables. The day was coming to a close.

Thulani gazed down upon a couple who stopped to kiss. He watched how the man held the woman's head with both hands as she pulled herself into him. Even if they had felt his eyes, they would not have cared. From above them he could see that the world around the two did not exist.

Caught up in this couple, their kiss, and thinking about what drew people to be entwined so, Thulani was suddenly surprised by a legion of wings flapping about him.

One by one, five rock doves descended on him, their pink feet touching down on his arms and shoulders; the nine other birds stopped at his feet.

Of his birds, he loved Yoli and Dija best, two of three snowy hens he found as squabs on his roof. Yoli was the first to recognize him as a "mother," and Dija followed her lead. Their sister, Esme, however, was indifferent to his attention. Of all his birds, she would be the one to run off with another flock.

His treasured cocks, Bruno and Tai-Chi, were brothers with identical black wing stains whom Thulani could easily tell apart. Bruno was bold, a leader, and Tai-Chi, the graceful one, was proud of his wingspan. Both birds had become his when they followed Esme to the rooftop one evening, but they had eventually mated with her sisters.

These were the only birds he had bothered to name. The three hens, the cocks, and their brood were simply "my birds." Truer friends did not exist. In the two years since Thulani had become owner and caretaker of his flock, there had been no discord, no change in routine, and, in spite of Esme's iffiness, no defections. His birds needed him to free them in the morning; he needed them to return before nightfall. Only when they died would they leave him.

In an act of dominance Bruno hopped from Thulani's shoulder to his head. Thulani grabbed Bruno's feet and carefully pried the bird's talons from his dreadlocks. "Stop showing off for Yoli. I know she's yours."

He threw Bruno up to the sky, then flung the others perched on his arms airborne as well. This was how his birds began their chasing game—running, hopping, and flying in circles around the roof. Each bird aimed for Thulani, to land on his shoulders, arms, or head.

Bruno wanted his head, but Thulani swerved, missing

those pink feet. He twisted, turned, waved his arms, and ducked. He could not shake Bruno or Tai-Chi, nor could he resist his hens.

When he tired or they tired, or when Shakira yelled up from the apartment window, "Cut the mischief!" he unlatched the door of the dovecote so they could roost.

"Home," he said in response to their cooing and flapping. "Home."

On his word they gathered to be let into the dovecote, an improvement on the avocado crate from Yong Moon's Fresh Fruits. The crate had served Yoli, Dija, and Esme as squabs but would not do as the three sisters grew into voluptuous hens that attracted other birds to the rooftop. In shop class he had made a bigger home with a lock and a swinging door. He had enjoyed building the dovecote and was at ease with a hammer.

"Home, Dija; home, Yoli; home, Bruno," he coaxed, until all hopped into the dovecote to roost.

Only one hen, Esme, lingered. Esme refused to breed, which went against the very nature of a hen. He'd watch his cocks do the mating dance, puff their necks, bob their heads in and out, and hop to one side, only to be spurned by Esme, who took the role of coquette too far, never allowing any to catch her. Even though Esme had attracted many male pigeons, a mourning dove, and a seagull, Yoli and Dija were responsible for increasing the brood.

"Home, Esme."

The lone hen stood her ground.

Thulani made kissing noises at her. This wouldn't do. He knelt and held out his hand filled with seeds, which caused a stir in the dovecote. Still, Esme showed no interest. She preferred to roost under the ledge where she and her sisters had been found, although the dovecote was kept clean and the water bowls were filled.

"Don't make me come and get you."

Esme tried to hop away. Thulani seized her, his thumb firmly planted against her beating heart. He grabbed her body before her wings could open. "It's better when you cooperate," he said, and dropped her into the box, then flipped the latch.

The July air began to cool. Thulani sat on the tarred roof next to his birds, his baggy T-shirt pulled over raised knees. Each pair, Yoli and Bruno, Dija and Tai-Chi, and others settled wing to wing. Even Esme recovered from the indignation of having been handled and joined in the low cooing.

"I *will* build a bigger home," he told his brood. "I will, I will, I will."

Lulled by the calm of murmuring birds, Thulani stayed on his roof well past midnight on summer nights like this. It was his refuge from Truman and Shakira and their desire to "man him up" for all his sixteen years.

Here on his roof he had the waning sun, a cooling breeze, his birds, and eventually, when night pulled down, a place to lay his head. Now that his birds had cooed themselves to sleep, he put on his headphones to pipe in the old-style reggae his mother used to blast and his father once sang. With this music, the pattern of stars, the peace within him, he closed his eyes and hung in the summer cool. Only then could he indulge himself in a dream where his head lay in the lap of a girl he did not know, just to smell her, feel the scratch of her long nails against his neck and chest, look into her eyes.

During the time he dreamed of her, he learned what he could not do. He could not fix on her face too strongly, for she would turn into other things. He could not imagine them elsewhere, say, in his bed, for the bed would smother them, or at school, for she would be swallowed by the crowd. She and he could be together only on his roof, his head in her lap as her nails drew patterns over his body. As long as he knew this, she would stay with him and he would have a place to rest his—

A scream.

Where from?

His dream girl fled. His eyes popped open, and his hand flew up against the dovecote. He removed the headphones and set aside his phone. Was it a cat trying to get at his birds? No. A cat couldn't climb up to the

6

roof. And the scream was human.

He checked his birds. They were shaken, but more so from his hand banging the cage.

"It's okay, it's okay."

There. Again. The scream.

Thulani was now on his feet, crouching low. He crept to the edge of the roof and looked down in the direction of the alley. In the dark he could see the Dumpster. Three figures were on the ground, eclipsed but not completely hidden by the Dumpster. He moved to the far right side to get a better angle. He saw them, out in the open, across the street in the alley. One guy, his pants down to his ankles, was on top of a woman. The other guy knelt by her head, holding her down while the first guy pumped her with his body.

Thulani stayed low, crouching and watching. When the one on top struck her, Thulani flinched to avoid the blow.

Move. Do something.

Vans passed by. A woman who had to have seen crossed the street.

Do something. *Something.*

The guy stopped pumping her. The other guy repositioned himself, maybe to hold her down better. Then the one on top, doing it, raised his arm and punched her in the face.

Thulani sprang tall. *"Hey, you!"*

The two guys stood and looked to the roof.

Thulani left his birds and The Wailers. He ran through the roof door, down the attic steps in a leap, down two flights of steps—"THULANI!"—past the blob that was his sister-in-law, and out into the street in a matter of seconds, his heart bursting through his chest. They had a knife to slice him up, a gun to shoot him full of lead. What did he have? One hundred and forty pounds of almost man, heart thumping through his chest, lungs pressing against his ribs.

He shot down the block, across the street, and into the alley. Die or be beaten, he had to do what he could for her.

His heart and lungs oozed out of his ears, but he was ready to face them. When he got there, to his relief the two had fled. He was alone in the alley, except for her.

He approached her carefully. She was alive but not fully conscious. He could also see that she wasn't a woman but a girl, like any girl he'd go to school with.

They had left her with her legs still open and no clothes on, except for ripped panties at her ankles. Her top, bright and pink with skinny straps, had been torn from her body. Her plum-colored nipples were sticking out. Her vagina, a crushed rose, was fully exposed, its petals dripping blood. Her face had been messed up. One eye was swollen shut, and her lip was busted.

Although he had been with her for only ten or fifteen seconds, it seemed longer. He didn't know what to do next. Should he leave her? Get help? Cover her? What? What?

Finally he knelt over the girl, realizing he'd have to touch her.

Maybe she felt him breathing. He was breathing awfully hard. She stirred, although her eyes remained closed. When he tried to touch her shoulder, to let her know he was there, she thrashed about like something wild, discovering the power of her legs.

"I'm not them! I'm not them! They're gone," he said, tolerating her open palm slaps. "They're gone."

This would not calm her. Still with eyes shut, she reached out for a piece of him, just to hit him.

"I'm not them!" he repeated loudly. Finally her arms died in the air, and her legs lost their power. "Look, girl. I live right there. My sister-in-law can tend to you."

"No-no-noooo!" She flung her arms in the direction of his voice. Her eyes were still closed.

Had she come out of the house like this? A top and no clothes?

He took off his oversize T-shirt, a shirt he wouldn't let Shakira borrow.

The girl was in no shape to help herself. He would have to touch her, sit her up, put the shirt on her, if she'd

9

let him. Or if he could get past her bruises, her gashes, her blood, her belly, her titties. He wanted to turn away, but he could not avert his eyes.

She struggled to raise herself. He lifted her into a sitting position, shoulders first. As he anticipated, she fought him. He did his best to slip the T-shirt over her head and guide her arms into the holes, while she wrenched her torso and spun her arms out and cursed him.

He had held frightened squabs but had never handled anything as delicate as this girl. He wanted to be gentle as he helped her to her feet, but she fought everything he did for her.

He didn't know what to do with her panties. One side was ripped completely. She could not bend to pull them up. When he tried to pull them up over her thighs, she screamed at him in words he didn't understand. He let them drop to the ground.

Her legs were weak. One foot turned in, and both legs shook. He knew that she would fall with her first step and that she would hit him if he tried to help her. He grabbed her arm anyway. She slapped his hand, as he knew she would.

He refused to let go.

"I know you're hurting, girl, but don't hit me. Don't hit me. I'm not them."

She took two steps, then paused. He reached out to give her balance. She hit him again, in spite of what he had told her. What could he do but bear her blows?

When they reached the end of the block, she stopped, then leaned into him, allowing him to support her. She opened her one good eye as best she could and looked around.

"Where you live? I'll take you."

"No. I'm fine." Her accent was thick. "I can go."

"Can't leave you, girl."

Since she wasn't talking, all he could do was let her guide them at her pace, taking ten minutes to complete each city block. Anyone still on stoops stared as they passed. He saw heads behind shaded windows, and he wondered what they thought with their mouths and eyes wide open.

When they turned on Franklin Avenue, the girl kept saying, "Okay, okay." He figured they were near her house. She turned to him and said sharply, "Now, go!" and pushed him away.

He wouldn't leave her alone and said, "You go in first; then I'll go." Before she could protest, the door opened. A woman too old to be her mother stood in the crack of the door before opening it wide. She snatched the girl inside, screamed in what he thought was Creole, and slammed the door.

He feared for the girl. He stood and waited for a sign that she would be all right.

The scolding ended with a slap. Then another. He

pressed himself to the door. The girl was sobbing and trying to explain. He had to get her out of there. Take her to the hospital, the police, or his house. He had to do something. He banged on the door.

"Girl? Girl, you all right in there?"

There was no answer.

Thulani was set to charge through the door when it swung open. The old woman came at him, yelling obscenities and waving his T-shirt as if it were a torch. He backed away, and she threw it at his chest.

The girl's voice pleaded in words he did not understand. She was telling the woman that he was not one of them.

It didn't matter. The old woman, still brandishing her fist, only knew what she saw. He with his filthy clothes on the girl's beaten-down body. Blood on her face, down her legs. He standing before her as if he had a right to be there.

Thulani backed away until he was running, in which direction it didn't matter. To the heads that looked out of windows, and to those who ventured outside to catch the action, he was guilty.

TWO

Thulani walked fast. Then he ran, down blocks, across avenues, even if they took him farther away from Eastern Parkway. Away from his house. His rooftop. His birds. He simply ran, stopping twice to mop his face, around his eyes with the T-shirt, the one the old woman had thrown at him, the one he had struggled to put on the raped girl's body. It didn't help. Wiping would not stop the pictures that played before him. Running could not put any bit of it behind him. Everywhere he turned masks followed him, vivid and distorted. He ran and ran but couldn't shake those sounds, those pictures. The scream, birds fluttering, the punch, one guy on top of her, the other holding her down, another punch—he still ducked—blood streaming from a busted lip, a closed eye, purple and swollen, plum-colored nipples, opened legs, the crushed rose, more blood, arms whirling, hands slapping, mad-crazy eyes of the old woman.

When he thought he would scream or lose his mind, he heard his mother's voice say, "Still yourself."

Thulani slowed to a trot, then a brisk walk, and none too soon. Up ahead he made out the distinct crawl of a blue-and-white in the next block. Spending his days on his rooftop did not make him ignorant of the streets below. He had seen enough to know how to carry himself and was determined to pass without being stopped by cops looking for a suspect.

The patrol car broke left on Nostrand. Thulani slid his hands into his pockets and tried to walk casually in case he was being watched. This was not easy, as he felt he looked guilty to anyone who saw him. Especially to the girl who would not stop hitting him, the old woman who cursed him in her language, and to the eyes that peeped out from behind curtains. Guilty.

She had to know that he had watched. That he could have been there thirty seconds sooner. That maybe she hadn't had to take that last punch. Her eye wouldn't be swollen, her lip busted up. She wouldn't have had to take so much from them if he had come down off the roof at her first scream. Why else would she continue to hit him when he told her to stop?

He was exhausted but not ready to come home.

Home was where he settled, and he was far from doing that. He took President Street, which was still lively with people, then walked two blocks, where there was no one. When his head began to clear somewhat, and the images that haunted him were not as sharp, one thought occurred to him: They're still out there. They had to have seen him, even if it was dark.

Thulani turned into Kingston, then thought, What makes you think they're not on Kingston?

He turned down Bedford.

What makes you think they're not on Bedford? They could be packing. If they could rape her, they could just as easily shoot me.

Then he heard it again: "Still yourself."

Thulani turned up Prospect Place and told himself, What will be, will be. If he had to step to them, he would. He had no one to back him up besides his brother, Truman, and Thulani didn't carry anything to defend himself. For all the good it did him, he had fourteen birds on a rooftop and, to his surprise, some heart.

Thulani returned to his block on Eastern Parkway, back to everything familiar. Even so, he could not go inside his house. He was drawn to the alley and had to see the place where it happened. He looked down upon the spot where he had found her, knelt, and touched the rough ground where she had lain on her back. Though he could not see it, he knew her blood was on the street, perhaps where he ran his hand.

To look at it, a strip between a Chinese takeout place and a barbershop, there was no trace of a crime scene. Just a place from which you'd naturally turn your gaze. A place where men took a piss in broad daylight and sanitation workers collected garbage from the Dumpster in the early hours.

Even though he was not one to throw himself before people, he felt he should tell someone that a girl had been raped where he stood. But whom would he tell? Could he open his mouth and have sense come out? All through school teachers had implored him to speak up or speak clearly. Talking was not his favorite thing.

He stood up and dusted off the grit from his hands on his shorts. It was then that he saw some figure billowing up from the ground on the side of the Dumpster. He approached it carefully, for it seemed alive. Thulani grabbed the moving thing. His fingers discovered it was merely a piece of cloth.

The thin material slid through his fingers like silk, but it wasn't silk. It was a fine cotton. Almost sheer. He couldn't imagine why this fine cloth had been thrown away. When he held it up to the sky, he could see by the way the bottom danced in the breeze that it was a skirt.

Instantly he knew it was hers. He thought it was the kind of thing she would wear, though he did not know her at all. He pictured her wearing it.

He opened the skirt fully. It was a free-flowing skirt that was tied, not zippered or buttoned. The tie, a simple strip, had been ripped, yet managed to hang on to the body of the skirt by a few loose threads. He looked about. Someone could be watching him. He shook the street off the cloth and rolled it into a tight loaf that he held under his arm. It was time to go home.

Upon seeing him, Shakira, his sister-in-law, let out a gasp, an exaggerated one. "Ya look a sight!"

He shrugged but thought, Got to get past her.

Shakira did not mean to let him pass. She stood, her belly huge, and legs a big *A* before him. "And what do ya mean, chargin' through heah wild and crazy, scarin' poor Old Dunleavy to his grave?"

Mr. Dunleavy, a countryman from Thulani's mother's village, was the tenant in the first-floor apartment. He had been a retired photographer for many years when Thulani's mother rented to him ten years ago. His mother was fond of saying, "He knew me before my parents were born." Now Old Dunleavy was decrepit. Thulani laughed inwardly at Shakira's concern for their tenant. Both she and Truman had plans for that apartment as soon as the boneyard claimed Old Dunleavy.

"The food is put away. You'll have to fix your plate if ya want to eat."

Shakira waited for some reply, the usual thing he'd say about her half cooking. All he wanted was to get away from her.

"Mnot hungry," he said, taking a big step to get around her. He could see she was a face full of questions and she wanted to talk.

"What's that you got there?" She spoke to his back. He wouldn't turn around.

It was easier when Truman wasn't on night shift because then Shakira had no use for Thulani. She and Truman would sit at the kitchen table and dream their dreams. Shakira was having some sort of difficulties with her pregnancy and was trapped in the house.

Thulani closed and locked his door by wedging the backrest of his chair underneath the knob. He fell into his bed with the cloth still tightly in his grasp. He lay on his back fingering the cloth, thinking that it had been tied around her body. The fine cotton cloth.

He had touched her. The girl. In fifteen or twenty seconds he had seen what girls hold secret, though she did not invite him. Or them. And he had her skirt. The torn cloth. In his bed.

He took the cloth and unfurled it from the tight roll, then spread it into a full rectangle on his bed. It was beautiful. An indigo sea, streaks of violet, drops of turquoise in bolder drops of gold. He ran his hands along the fabric, searching for the girl who wore it. To picture her in it, he had to see it fully open. He took two nails and a hammer from his bottom drawer and began to nail the cloth to the wall facing his bed.

"Thulani! What's that noise?"

He ignored Shakira.

She jiggled the doorknob but could not get in.

"Thulani! What are ya doing?"

"Leave me alone" is what he said, but it came out in a mumble.

"Thulani, open."

He blasted his stereo. Some Wyclef Jean. Finally she gave up.

Shakira didn't really care, he reasoned. She was doing what she thought her role as woman of the house called for. He wished she'd do it elsewhere and leave him alone. He wanted no words tonight.

He hammered the last nail; then he lay in his bed to admire the skirt. He was so struck with the cloth he couldn't sleep. At the Dumpster he could not fully appreciate the colors. The indigo. The turquoise. The violet and gold. But now, in his bed with the lights turned off, he saw the design, which was the pattern of a peacock in full fan. Thulani could not take his eyes off the colors. And in the semi-darkness it seemed as if a hundred golden eyes of the peacock all stared back.

THREE

With the exception of one recurring event, every Wednesday was like every Monday, was like every Tuesday. That Wednesday Thulani rose, showered, stepped into a pair of baggy Bermuda shorts, then went out onto his roof to be with his birds. Instead of sharing last night's dreams with them, he asked aloud, "What should I do about her? It's Wednesday."

For the past five weeks since that night, he had spotted her, the raped girl, coming down Eastern Parkway every Wednesday at eleven-twenty, by the bank clock. The first time he saw her, he felt a strong urge to get to the street, just as he had done that night. Unfortunately, like that night, he couldn't move. He simply let her pass and watched her until she slipped into what had to be

Nostrand Avenue. Then he'd stay on his roof and listen to music, stare at cloud formations, or design bigger dovecotes in his head, until the bank clock showed one-fifteen and she returned from wherever she went.

He knew she would be passing through. He wondered how she was. If she was okay. He wanted to ask her, face-to-face, "Are you okay?"

He looked to his birds for advice, resolved to take any hint as a sign and act upon it. Yoli and Dija cooed sympathetically, but this told him nothing. Tai-Chi demonstrated the graceful art of diving for last night's pizza crust but was cut off by Bruno, who swooped down and snatched it.

"What, you crazy?" he asked Bruno. "I'd scare her."

The fact remained, Bruno had the pizza crust.

Thulani turned to Esme, who, as usual, was off by herself. "Hey, Es-may, hey, Esemaay. Hey, girl."

Esme hopped away.

"Don't be like that. Tell me what to do, what to say, you being a woman."

Esme did not want to be bothered. She perched on the antenna.

Thulani waved her off. His birds could not help him, and he had detained them long enough. He watched them fly away under Bruno's lead, banking right, left, and out of sight.

It was early yet. He had time before she would appear. He went inside to take breakfast. His brother, Truman, had come in from his shift and was off to bed. This left him with Shakira, who was stirring a pot of thick, lumpy, whole-grain porridge. She ate these concoctions whether she liked them or not for the sake of her unborn child. Natural foods were better for the baby, according to Shakira. He grabbed a bowl, his box of Cap'n Crunch, or "processed sugar," and sat at the table.

"Correct me if I'm mistaken," Shakira began, "but I did not sleep with you last night."

Thulani grunted at her, rather than say the "Good morning, sistah dear," she wanted. He watched her pour the glop into a bowl and thought, Vile. She read his face well but joined him at the table nonetheless. He would be content to eat in silence, although Shakira would never let him get away without conversation, sitting face-to-face. She swallowed a spoonful of her porridge, took a moment to clear her mouth, then asked, "Ya have plans?"

He never took this to be a serious question. She always asked this, and his answer was always the same: "Naw" or a head shake.

"Ya let this whole summer go by, no work, no studies, no friends."

"So."

"You're not a child, Thulani. Ya should be planning.

Doing. Thinking about college."

He poured more milk and cereal into his bowl.

"Ya drink too much cow's milk." With Shakira it was always some new thing she got hold of from books and magazines. She had come to their house touting goat's milk as "the righteous milk." Then it was soy milk. Now rice milk.

He knew what to do in this situation. "Could you be looved?," a favorite of his father's. His music was there in his head when he needed to drown out Shakira. "Don't let them change you." He crunched loud, bobbing his head while she talked on. At this point The Wailers were much too mellow. He switched to Shabba.

Shakira had to know he had left her, although this did not discourage her. After nearly three years of Shakira in the house he knew her litany cold: He was too much into himself. He sat on his roof, talked to birds, got blacker by the sunloads, ate Cap'n Crunch, had no ambitions, no girlfriend, yah, yah. She could talk and talk. None of these things was on his mind. He thought only of her, the girl, and that she would be passing by in yet another hour.

Thulani washed and dried his bowl, watched some TV, then went back up to his roof. It was ten minutes past eleven. He knelt at the edge of the roof, in his "waiting for her" position. He still had not figured out what he would do or say, but he knew he would do something. Perhaps come down off the roof, tap her on the shoulder, and say, "Girl, I've been thinking about you. Are you all right?"

He played this back to himself to get a feel for her reaction. As he tried to picture her expression and what she might say, he realized he had only a distorted face to go by. True, he had filled in his dream girl's face with her face, but he had wiped away her blood and healed her scars.

This made him wonder if she had healed in five weeks. Could he look at her without pausing on her scars? Would she recognize him and thank him for rescuing her, or would she fall apart?

He began to think that trying to talk to her was a bad idea. That maybe the best thing to do was leave her alone. Let her be. Hadn't she been through enough? He was about to step away from the edge of the rooftop but then saw her coming down Eastern Parkway, her head and chest high, her gait proud and undaunted as she passed the alley. She carried a backpack and wore a long skirt that swayed as she walked. He imagined it was much like the skirt nailed to his wall, made of fine silky cotton, except for its single color, bright marigold. As he watched her walking swiftly with her head high, it puzzled him that she was not in hiding and that her colors were so bold.

He followed her down the long block with his eyes, not realizing that he had crept along to the other end of the rooftop. It was when she disappeared down Nostrand Avenue that he told himself he might never get another chance to talk to her. He ran inside the apartment, past a startled Shakira, and was on Eastern Parkway running after her. He stopped to catch his breath at Nostrand Avenue and to see if he could spot her. There were only a few bystanders at the bus stop; not one of them was the girl.

She could have turned on Lincoln Place or gone into a store on St. Johns, but which one? Thulani looked into shops along the block. Although he didn't know her, he couldn't imagine her going for pizza before noon. He didn't glance inside Ayoka's Hair Braiding, for braids didn't require a weekly visit. Besides, she wore her hair pulled up on her head, never braided. He did glance inside the real estate office, the money transfer place, and the music store. No girl in a yellow-gold skirt. He tried the flower shop, this time going inside.

"Yeah, boss?"

"Just looking," Thulani said. "For someone."

The florist's eyes said, Do you see anyone here? Thulani backed out of the store, accidentally kicking a potted plant.

Why was he running after her? This was crazy. He was crazy. Obviously she was all right. She had filed her police report and gotten tested. She didn't need him to ask how she was, remind her of that night, or stare at her scars. She had passed by with her head held high, not offering the alley a side glance. She didn't hide in dark colors. She didn't need him to rescue her.

He decided to turn back, and there she appeared in her skirt, bright and yellow. She had stepped out of a shop on the opposite side of the street and tucked something, perhaps a small bag, into her backpack and continued down Nostrand.

He crossed the street to get a better look at the shop she had come out of. It was a store with Chinese characters painted on the door, and a sign propped in the window that read CHINESE HERBS AND MEDICINE, ACUPUNCTURE ON PREMISES.

He didn't want to go inside; he just wanted to know what it was all about. Thulani pressed his face against the window but saw no one. On the counter sat a mortar and pestle and a set of measuring scales, much smaller than those used in grocery stores. Behind the counter were cabinets with about fifty little drawers, each one marked with Chinese characters.

When the shopkeeper, a middle-aged Chinese woman in a white lab coat, appeared from the back room, Thulani stepped away.

What did she want with Chinese herbs? Why did it take five or ten minutes to prepare? Where did she go next, and why did it take an hour before she returned to Eastern Parkway?

He could see her up ahead. There was a block and a half between them. He took one step, another, and a broad Mother-May-I in her direction. Her skirt movement hypnotized him. The dance of her lean and sensual body made him forget she was a rape victim; she was a girl whose skirt swayed with the sea. Not only did she pull *him* with her motion, but other men turned to watch her walk by.

Thulani wondered if she wore no bra and if her nipples showed against the fabric of her top. Picturing her body in detail made him erect, something that happened seemingly all the time. Girls had aroused him before, but this was different. She was flesh. Warm. Angry. And he did not have to imagine her. He had seen her. Touched her.

Then she stopped abruptly, and he froze, expecting her to turn around. Just as abruptly as she stopped, she continued, only now at a slightly faster pace.

What now? he thought. Run after her? Then what? He only wanted to know she was all right. This was what he told himself as he walked faster to keep up with her. After all, he had rescued her. Or had she rescued him? Because of her, that awful night, he had run out into the world to aid someone, without fear.

She vaulted up the steps to some building in the next

block. As he approached, he saw it was St. Augustine's, a Catholic church. A statue of St. Augustine, a black missionary in a long robe, held out welcoming arms. Thulani wiped his hands on his Bermudas, wiped his sweaty forehead and face on his shirt, and went up the steps to the Catholic church. He entered the church, but he did not want her to see him just yet, so he stepped into a little room off to the side. The entrance to the room was draped in a maroon velvet curtain. There was a dark screen before him that separated his little room from yet another. Before him were the words "Bless me, Father, for I have sinned" in English, Spanish, and French.

If he remained quiet, he would not be discovered. He would wait and peer out of the velvet curtain until the service was over. When she came out, he would talk to her.

Excluding his brother's wedding, it had been years since he had attended a church service. His mother was Episcopalian. He too was Episcopalian, back when he attended Holy Trinity on Fulton. That was three Easters ago. His mother was no longer with him, and he hadn't been Episcopalian ever since. His brother had become a Rasta, the creed of his father. Now Truman was married and a transit worker. Those were his religions. Work and Shakira. He seemed less and less a brother.

• • •

The aroma of incense that drifted from the altar found his hiding place. Through the slightly pulled-back drapes he watched a black priest say mass to the girl and mostly elderly men and women. The priest spoke and made hand gestures, raising his fingers to his forehead, lips, and heart. The parishioners responded in kind. Thulani tried to follow what was being said but could not, for the priest and the parishioners spoke in what he thought was French.

"Haitian," he said aloud. "She's Haitian."

He watched her make the sign of the cross, kneel and rise several times. When they sang hymns, he picked out her voice, which rose above those of the old people, the organist, and the priest. It was a voice that wore bright colors. She then took communion, her pride replaced with humility. When the mass was over, and the priest had left, she went to the altar of candles, took dollar bills from her backpack, and put them in a box. He watched as she lit the tallest candle and knelt, her head bowed, her back curved, legs ending in sandaled feet, making a number two in profile. She rose, dipped her fingers into a ceramic fount, and made the sign of the cross, touching her forehead, above her abdomen, then both sides of her chest. She repeated an anointing of her abdomen and pelvis—something no one else did. She then took a small vessel of some kind, dipped it into the fount, capped it, and placed it in her backpack. Each action she carried out with her head lowered.

Thulani had to get out of there. He slipped out of the confessional and left the church. She would be outside within seconds. While waiting for her in the parking lot, he had made up his mind. No more following her. When she came down the church steps, he would walk up to her and offer to walk her home.

She was awfully fast, or he wasn't as brave as he thought. She sped right past him and was halfway down the block by the time he saw her.

Thulani walked fast. His legs were longer than hers, and his stride was greater. He lost sight of her in front of him and was practically on top of her when she turned around.

"You!" she screamed. Even then her accent was thick.

He was stunned, tongue-tied. Before he could explain or apologize or ask if she was all right, she took off, the backpack bouncing against her. She never looked back.

Thulani vowed to leave her alone and to let her die in his mind. He would no longer care if she was all right, and he would stop filling in his dream girl's face with her face. Her prayers, candles, and Chinese herbs were silly next to his vow.

Before he fell asleep that night, he faced the skirt nailed to his wall and said, "To hell with her."

FOUR

A hot one is what the DJ on the radio promised. Hotter than Hades, damp like mop water. Thulani felt it in the early morning as he watched his birds fly off. He felt the thickness surround him when he looked down on what would be, in an hour, sheer madness. Police stationed barricades along Eastern Parkway. Vendors set up their tents and tables while revelers slowly filled the streets. Madness.

Carnival in Brooklyn—or, as the newspapers called it, the West Indian Day Parade—was nothing like carnival in Jamaica. Back in Jamaica, carnival went on for days and nights. Calypso, socca, and reggae called dancers out into the streets. People gathered for parties in every home. It was a happy time. Even Daddy stopped working long enough to throw Thulani up on his shoulders to watch the festivities.

Up on Daddy's shoulders was a place reserved for Thulani alone. He played with Daddy's long dreads and stuck out his tongue at Truman down below. Riding high on Daddy's shoulders made him tall, tall like the men on stilts.

Sometimes he thought it had all been a dream. Being too little to climb trees with Truman, being chased by a neighbor's goat, or looking up at green hills, as high and far as his eyes could see. Even Daddy, tall and soft-spoken, always smelling of black licorice, seemed a dream man.

If he had been older than three when he, Mommy, and Truman left Jamaica, he would still have his father's ways and voice cut firmly into his memory. He envied Truman for having known Daddy and for showing off the things Daddy taught him, such as how to start up a car, change a fuse, or pound a nail square on with his hammer.

In spite of the photographs of Daddy stationed throughout their home, and all of Mommy's recollections, Daddy remained clouded in smoke and green hills. He had been told that Daddy was "a fine carpenter" and that he built the best cabinets, tables, and coffins in St. Catherine. He had been told that Daddy was the youngest of eight sons and, like Thulani, was his mother's favorite. He knew a great many things about his father, though none of these things brought him closer to his memory. It was only at carnival time that the image of Daddy, the feel of his hair, the licorice chew stick in his mouth, the *clomp-ca-lomp* of his work boots, and his singing as he worked, became clear.

When they first came to Brooklyn, Auntie Desna, who was not a relation but a woman from Mommy's village, took them into her home on Bedford Avenue. In those early days Thulani stayed posted at the door, watching for those work boots to *ca-lomp* through the door. Either Mommy led him away from the door and said, "Daddy will follow," or Truman would hit him for behaving like a baby.

That summer Auntie Desna told them about the West Indian Day Parade. She promised them a good time, saying the parade "will bring you back home." When Thulani saw and heard the familiar things, the men on stilts, the steel drums, the reggae, the dancers in mas, he was sure Daddy would come to him, as he always had, out of the green hills. Year after year Thulani searched the crowd to see if Daddy was out there, caught in the pushing and dancing. Many a time he tore himself from his mother or from Truman to go running after some dreadlocked man, only to be disappointed. The last time he ran after a stranger, Mommy grabbed him and shook him and said firmly—for she never meant to repeat herself—"I begged Daddy to come, but he wouldn't leave. Once Daddy stuck in his safe place, he'll not budge."

Daddy had sent money from time to time and occasionally a card for birthdays. He had even sent Thulani toy animals that he carved from scraps of wood. But Thulani could not remember the last time he had actually spoken to his father. And that was what he wanted. To hear his father's voice.

Thulani looked down on the madness, determined to stay above it. The two times that he felt compelled to come down were both because of her, and he would never be so compelled again. Not after she had run from him when all he wanted was to . . .

He wasn't sure.

He tried to let the girl go. Stop thinking about her. But everything about her opened questions in his mind. What could he do? Nothing. Not even if she went through life thinking he was someone she had to run from.

He couldn't blame her. He had followed her that Wednesday. He had paced his distance so he could enjoy the sway of her hips as she walked down the street. He had hidden himself in the church so he could watch her pray. When he worked up the courage to tap her and speak, she had caught him.

He thought of writing her a letter to explain. Apologize. He thought if she read his words, she could hear his voice and know that he meant her no harm. It would be a deep letter. He would compose his thoughts. Find something that would reach her. Put her at ease, if that was possible. Then he would write neatly. Stick the letter in her mailbox and walk away.

This sounded good until he realized that he did not know her name or where to begin. In his head he said,

Girl,
Dear Girl,
Dear Girl Who Was Raped,
I'm the one who helped you that night.
I'm the one who you hit.
I'm the one who followed you.

No. Not a letter. He had to talk to her. Let her look into his eyes. See that he didn't mean to frighten her. More important, he had to see himself in her eyes and know she didn't think the worst of him.

"Bird bwai!"

It was Shakira. In his room, at his window, trespassing on his peace.

"Thulani, don't make me come up there."

He sighed, feeling the weight of her on him. If she later complained of aches from the stair climbing, he wouldn't hear the end of it from Truman. Before he could get up to answer her, she was standing in the doorway that led to the roof, her arms folded over her belly.

"What?"

"Take down my table."

"Down where? In that?" He meant the carnival mob. "Not me."

"I've been working all summer on my tings," she whined, a sure sign that she would tell Truman. "I have a friend holding my spot. They can't hold it forever, you know."

He was comfortable where he was. He didn't want to face her, let alone answer.

"Ya hear me, Thulani?"

"It's too crazy," he said.

All summer long Shakira had sewn pillows and dolls like those from Jamaica, Trinidad, Barbados, and the Dominican Republic to sell for ten dollars apiece. She called it extra income, but Thulani knew it was busywork while she was housebound. Even Truman did not like the idea of her fighting among the crowd, but she seemed determined to be in the midst of the parade.

Thulani would have been quicker about helping her

if it weren't for her attitude. It was the way that she pro-claimed herself woman of his mother's house that made him slow to move. It was her expectation that he should come when she called or answer every question she put to him. She was his brother's wife, but nothing to him.

"I'll tell Truman."

Still no reply. As far as he was concerned, she could stand there all she wanted. Threaten. Whine. Stomp. Go into labor, for all he cared. He wasn't going.

"Fine," she yelled up. "Mtakit mdamnself!"

He threw a pebble that hit the TV antenna. That was all he needed—for Shakira to tell Truman how she struggled down flights of stairs with her table, then fought through the crowds.

If Truman had married Shakira to take care of things when Mommy left, it was not necessary. Mommy had taught Thulani everything. He could steam doctorfish, make oxtail stew and dumplings. He could wash clothes to perfection and take needle and thread to any mend-ing job.

Shakira, on the other hand, was hardly a cook, although Truman ate with gusto everything she burned. She was a "neatener," not a scrubber like Mommy. If Thu-lani wanted the bathroom and kitchen sparkling clean, he had to do that himself.

In spite of the fact that Shakira seemed good for only reading and crowing, Mommy said she was perfect for Truman. When it was clear that they would marry, Mommy gave Truman her emerald ring from Daddy to offer as an engagement ring. To Shakira she turned over hand-sewn baby clothes, recipes, and stories that she had shared only with Thulani.

After almost three years Thulani had no choice but to accept that Truman loved Shakira. He had long given up complaining that Shakira overstepped her boundaries or that her cooking and housekeeping were so-so. Truman took her side in every matter. It was just easier for Thulani to stay on the roof with his birds.

He found Shakira loading her wagon with dolls when he came inside. She smiled but didn't bother to look at him. As he folded the legs of the card table, she could not let the opportunity pass and said, "You know what's good."

The parade was everything he had seen from the roof, except instead of being above the madness, he was surrounded by it. Sheer madness. He and Shakira were lucky to have a spot along the parkway to pitch the card table. There were twice as many vendors as last year. Stands with codfish cakes, coconut drinks, dolls, flags, and bootleg tapes lined the parade route. The streets were packed with parade-goers—dancing, milling, pushing, and buying.

Though he didn't want to be with her in all the chaos, he could not help but marvel at his sister-in-law. Determined to sell every doll and pillow, she was hardly meek about flagging down potential buyers. While she sold, Thulani fetched mountain springwater—"not distilled, not mineral"—and plates with samples from every other stand. When Shakira was low on change, Thulani went from table to table to break twenties. When she went to the portable toilets, he watched her table. As long as there was no lull, he didn't mind being there.

It became unbearable when after three hours only two dolls remained and passersby sped past Shakira's table. With no buyers to cajole, Shakira turned her talk to Thulani.

"That's a pretty cloth you have."

He pretended not to hear.

"On your wall," she said, begging a reaction, some telltale gesture that she could pounce on.

Heat rose up in him. She had no right to be among his things. To stick and prod him.

"Where did you get it?"

"Nowhere."

"A cloth like that had to come from somewhere."

She had no right.

With one sweep he knocked the dolls off the table.

"What! You crazy? Where you going? You have to help me."

He turned his back to her and was absorbed into the moving crowd. He could hear her calling after him. He wouldn't leave her there to struggle with the table and cart. He'd be back. He just had to step away from her at that moment. He wasn't ready to talk about the girl. Or her skirt. Or the alley. He certainly didn't want to hear Shakira's spin on it. Not while the girl was in his every thought.

He needed his stride to be wide and free, but no one step was his own. He was pushed into a group of female dancers in mas, their buttocks and breasts jutting out of scanty, sequined costumes. Their flesh surrounded him. One dancer shoved him. Someone kicked him. Another dancer teased him, shimmying her breasts at him and sticking out her tongue. He broke free of them and imagined himself running through the hills of his homeland until exhaustion washed away his rage and suffocation. Then he saw a trace of green cloth. Bright, bold, like the green parrots of the Amazon. He saw it as its wearer dashed across the parade route and was swallowed in the thick of the crowd ahead.

His mind raced. Was that the girl in one of those

skirts? This was his chance. He had to find her. He began to push through the crowd.

"Eh! You crazy?"

"Hey, bwai. Watch it."

He didn't care. He couldn't let her get away. He knew what he wanted. Her name. He had to know her name. She took up almost every thought in his head. He needed her name to go with his thoughts. And to talk to her. And maybe smell her. To be close to her for a minute. Everything in him stood up large. His heart, his voice, his longing. He could not let her go.

Although he lost sight of her green skirt up ahead, he had to believe she was there. He would have to swim through the throng, ten-man deep, just to reach her. His heart was beating in his ear. What would he say when he caught her?

He tried to see the back of her head, but it was impossible. The crowd was too dense. The people, all dancing, pushing, milling. He couldn't get through. He jumped up high, but the Jamaican float was passing through, its carnival priestess imploring the masses to jump up, jump up. He could not find the girl or her green skirt.

In his head he heard his mother say, "Still yourself. Just be still." He had to trust this voice. Even if he got to the girl, he couldn't just rush her. He would scare her.

He would have to do it right. Approach her carefully. Let her see him coming, if that was possible. Let her decide if she wanted to talk to him. If she ran from him again, then and only then would he let her go.

He made his way through a cluster of blue and yellow T-shirts. If he could only get around the next group, he would be in front of her. He couldn't see her too well, but he caught glimpses of the bright green skirt.

He somehow had to get ahead of her.

He saw his chance and ducked under a blue wooden police barricade and ran ahead. A police officer blew his whistle at him, but it was okay. He was now in front of her. He slipped back under the barricade before the police officer came and stood at a stand of figures carved from coconut skins. She would not miss him.

The Jamaican float pushed on, and its priestess took the crowd with it. Steel drums clanged in his heart as he waited.

She was coming, surrounded by friends. They had stopped to get a better glimpse of the oncoming Trinidadian float, and he feared she would cross to the other side of the street. But she didn't. She was headed for the table.

"Hey," he'd say, and nod as she passed by. If she didn't give him a rude look, he would know everything was all right, and one day, if not today, he could approach her.

She was coming. He had to be in her direct path, so he stepped out before her. As the people who surrounded the girl in the bold green skirt unpeeled themselves from her one by one, she caught his eye and smiled at him. But it wasn't her.

FIVE

The sun peeled open his eyes as he lay in his bed. He had overslept. He had no place to go but up to the roof and free his birds.

An hour earlier he would have slipped downstairs and eaten his cereal unnoticed. As it was, he could hear Shakira telling about the comedies and splendor of carnival to Truman in an excited patois. Thulani himself no longer spoke patois, thanks to a prekindergarten teacher, a strict Jamaican woman, who advised his mother to speak only proper English, if he was to succeed in school. This start-and-stop talking of trying to speak proper English confused him. He would raise his hand in class and speak, only to have his tongue cut off each and every time. It was easier to be quiet.

To enter the kitchen, Thulani stepped over Truman's legs, which were extended outward, a deliberate obstacle. Stepping over Truman was a "little brother" toll he paid, since Truman clearly would not move. Offering them both a morning greeting was yet another toll. They reminded him at every opportunity, We are your elders, not your equals.

He got his cereal and milk and sat at the table. Between Shakira's expanding belly and Truman's long legs, the room was too tight. Knowing Truman was watching, he poured his cereal, then scooped a handful into his pants pocket.

"There you go, feeding those birds with my food."

"Don't fuss with Thulani," Shakira defended, in a mock tone for sure. She was still fanning herself with the money she made at carnival. "I couldn't have sold my dolls without him."

He wouldn't give her the benefit of a smile. If he hadn't returned to help her pack up her table, she would be telling Truman how he had thrown a fit at her and knocked down her dolls.

She placed two ten-dollar bills in front of Thulani's bowl, waited for him to acknowledge her gift, then counted and re-counted over three hundred dollars with her stubby fingers.

Thulani felt their eyes preying on him, like a cat

waiting for a sparrow to make the wrong move. He wouldn't touch the money.

Shakira chattered on about the parade while she made out a deposit slip to their cherished savings account, the window of their dreams. Truman insisted that she treat herself to a dress or perfume with the money, but Shakira wouldn't hear of it. Every cent was going to their nest egg. Their dream house in New Jersey.

They weren't speaking to each other but to him: This is what responsible people do, Thulani. Save for the future. He ate his cereal.

Shakira drummed her nails on the table to get Thulani's attention. "Go collect the rent from Dunleavy. Take the rent and our carnival earnings straight to the bank."

With a mouth full of cornflakes he said, "Ask me."

"She just did." Truman was firm. End of discussion.

Thulani shook his head.

"And you might want to take a dollar or two from your earnings and deposit it to your savings account." She was trying to sound like Mommy.

He refused to look as if he were considering her suggestion. It did not matter. Truman held on to Thulani's savings book, and it would snow in hell before his brother let him see it, let alone draw from it. Having him ask for every dollar was how Truman kept him underfoot.

"You can't just spend, spend your money," Shakira

said. "You must put something away."

This was precisely why he was slow to pick up the money. If the twenty dollars was his money, then it was his alone to do as he pleased. If it was theirs, they should keep it.

Truman pointed to the bank envelope. "That's a lot of responsibility we're giving you," he told his brother. "A lot of trust."

Thulani put the bank envelope in his pocket but left the two tens on the table. It was not the first time he had deposited Dunleavy's rent check. They were making a big deal for no reason.

"There's a party at my sister's," Shakira said. "Come with us."

He looked up at her with his mother's almond-shaped eyes.

"My cousins will be there, and it will be nice. Plenty of food. Music. Dancing."

Shakira and Truman exchanged looks. They had been discussing him. Again. He did not have to actually hear these talks to know what was said. "Sixteen and no future, no plans, no friends." "Get him a job, a woman, and kill those birds. That will set him straight."

At Truman's urging, which consisted of a look, lips pursed in a kiss, and a slight turn of the head, Shakira left the room.

"Hey. You."

Thulani looked up.

"Shakira's been tellin' her cousins about you. Talkin' you up good."

He meant her female cousins. The ones his age. Thulani shrugged.

"You're sixteen, braa. Dead is dead."

Thulani cut a look into his brother.

"I no stuttah," Truman said. "Let go of Mommy. Live your life."

"She was our mother. I can't erase her."

"No one said erase," Truman said. "Just grow up. Be a man. Mopin' won't bring back Mommy. Mommy gone, Thulani. Mommy dead."

What did Truman know or feel? By the time Mommy left, Truman was twenty and had climbed out of his youth into manhood. He had met his wife-to-be and had passed the test for the Transit. He had only to deal with the grief of losing Mommy and not the pain of needing her.

From the time Mommy announced that she was flying home to Jamaica for a short while, Thulani had begged to go with her each and every day. He seemed to exhaust her, but she remained firm about leaving him behind. She had to visit Daddy alone. Thulani would come home another time. She said good-bye at the airport—nothing too emotional, just a kiss and a hug—and she was off to their home in St. Catherine, where the hills were covered with trees, and the rains poured down, the sun broke through the mountain peaks, and Daddy waited. There she spent three weeks with Daddy, while he cared for her and built her coffin.

Mommy always said she had three lives: her past life in Jamaica, life with her sons in Brooklyn, and the life to come. Thulani never sought to understand the riddles she spoke in. When he was thirteen, and his mother began to speak in riddles, he cared about video games, briefly for a girl who flirted with him in class, and about his music. Only Truman and Mommy knew that she was dying. Only they knew that this was a kiss good-bye.

There was no telephone in Daddy's house, so Thulani wrote letters to let his mother know he was no longer angry she had left him behind. How many letters she actually read he did not know. Truman let him mail those letters, make a Mother's Day gift, and talk of "when Mommy comes back" until one day Truman just said it: "Mommy died two weeks past."

Thulani had watched her get on the plane and watched the plane take off. It had not occurred to him that she would not return.

•   •   •

"Mommy had cancer, and she went home to die. That's it," Truman continued.

"You should have told me."

"And what could you do? What could I do? She was gone. Before our eyes."

Anger had Thulani by the throat. He didn't speak for a time. Then he said, "You knew good-bye was good-bye."

Truman stood up. He didn't have much use for this kind of talk. He said, "The party's at Shakira's sister. We're all going early to help out."

Shakira materialized to say, "And take a hot, hot bath. I don't want anyone smelling pigeon shit."

Only when Truman and Shakira both went to their bedroom did he take the twenty dollars. He went up to the roof and unlatched the crates. His birds had been locked in for too long.

He asked for their forgiveness and sprinkled the gold flakes he had in his pocket onto the tarp. "I'm gonna build you a dovecote like no other," he promised while they clamored for the cereal.

He watched them fly off into the final days of true summer. In a week he would be one of a thousand lost heads locked in school, roaming the halls. Already he mourned the warm kiss of the sun on his face, arms, and chest.

He knew he would not go to the party with Truman

and Shakira. The lure of good food, music, and Shakira's pretty cousins could not disguise what the gathering was about. An attempt to grow him up. Have him think family, earning, contributing, marrying one of those she-cousins one day soon, and taking root in a house in New Jersey with his brother and Shakira.

Thulani knocked on Mr. Dunleavy's door and waited. Dunleavy moved slowly, relying upon his walking stick, which Thulani could hear tapping against the floor.

Thulani dreaded collecting the rent. Mr. Dunleavy would never simply hand him the check and let him go. The old man always wanted to show Thulani an old camera or photographs of Jamaica. Mr. Dunleavy had made his living as a photographer, taking pictures for newspapers, magazines, and even postcards. The photographs covered his walls.

If Mr. Dunleavy did not try to interest Thulani in photography or Jamaica, he always spoke of Thulani's mother. That he had known her when she was a schoolgirl, no older than Thulani.

Mr. Dunleavy cracked the door ajar. Thulani thought, The snow came down hard on a man, an expression his mother used. Dunleavy's hair and mustache were completely white.

To Thulani's relief, Mr. Dunleavy had the rent check in his hand.

"Not feeling too well," Mr. Dunleavy said, giving him the check. "You run along."

Instead of going directly to the bank, he went to the big library at the edge of the park. He pulled two books from the shelves—one on carpentry and another on bird habitats. As he sank down in the stacks and flipped through pages of dovecote designs, he lost track of the bank, the party, the plane, and his mother.

He studied the architecture of these mostly open-faced cubbyholes and thought of ways to add a protective screen with a latch. He needed a door of some kind to lock his birds in at night. How else would he free them in the morning?

He returned the books to their shelves and left the library. It was after two-thirty. He had to cut through Prospect Park to make the deposit at Carver Federal. He couldn't dally at the fishpond, or linger over the orchids—orchids his mother said grew like weeds in her garden in St. Catherine.

He hurried along, thinking of the deposit envelope in his pocket. Then he stopped. Before him, cutting across the park, he saw a sway of color, a bouquet in the breeze. It was a skirt—lavender, yellow, green, and blue. This time he was not deceived by his eagerness. *It was her.*

S I X

Don't run, don't run, don't run, is what his heart said, each *thump-thump* a plea to both himself and to her. If he rushed her in all of his excitement, she would run. If she ran from him, he'd have to let her go, even if he never got to know her.

He tried to slow his pace, but she was too near. Sooner or later she would feel him behind her. He called out, "Hey!" louder than he intended, but she didn't turn around. He tried again. "Hey, girl in the—" He stopped, tongue-tied on those colors she wore. A rainbow of them. Still nothing. She had to know he meant her. There was no one else in the park but them.

He watched her. Her skirt billowed. Her hair was gathered on top of her head, which she held high. Just as he remembered from those Wednesdays from the roof. If she saw him and smiled, if she saw him and smiled . . .

He ran out of small steps. When he was abreast of her, but not too close, he said, "Please don't run."

She gave a side glance and said, "You." She was suddenly real, not the blur of a face he'd color in minus scars, but a face full of disdain and beauty that up close he could see he had gotten wrong.

"Look. I didn't mean to scare you that day."

Her eyebrows, thick and arched, said, Me, scared?

For nearly two months he had been rehearsing this moment. He had been sitting on his rooftop practicing his speech for Yoli and Dija; Esme didn't care. He had been lying on his bed in the dark, apologizing to the skirt nailed to his wall. Suddenly no words could be enough to offer this very real, angry girl whose quick, mad glances speared him. All he could do was walk with her and hope to find himself and say what he needed to say.

She cut another look at him and tossed her head. He loved her hair. It was thick and rippled like hair that had been braided and unbraided. In spite of that evil glance his first thought was to touch it.

"I don't like how you follow me," she said. "Everywhere I turn, there you are. What do you do—watch and watch me?"

He wanted to say no, but he didn't lie easily. He did watch her at every opportunity.

"*Stop* following me."

"I—I was going this way when I saw you coming across the park."

"Oh? And you was going to St. Augustine's? To get down on your knees? Say 'Hail Mary, don't put fruit in my womb?' Yeh?"

He was struck dumb by her and couldn't come quick enough. Everything about her threw him off. Her lips, her eyebrows, her hair, her blunt little nose.

When he couldn't answer, she gave him yet another look of disgust and walked away.

He stayed with her, which only annoyed her, but he had to speak now or forget it. "That day . . . at your church . . ."

She stopped.

"I'm sorry."

He waited for her to speak, to accept his apology, but she said nothing. Since she didn't walk away from him, he kept talking. "I don't want you to think the wrong thing about me. Ever since that night . . ." Her eyes stopped him cold. It was too late to take it back. "I—I'm just sorry. . . ."

"*Why?*" she snapped. "Did you do it?"

He shook his head no.

"Then keep your sorry."

Nothing was as it should have been. She was supposed to recognize him as her savior. They were supposed to be joined by that bad night like survivors of an airplane crash. In his dreams they embraced. She cried in his arms. He said everything was all right.

"I wonder about you," he said softly. "All the time."

"What you need to know?" Her fury spun out at him. She, the girl who knelt so humbly with her head lowered, was in his face. "You know everything of mines. You see everything of mines. What else you need to know?"

"That you're all right."

"I'm fine. See?" She twirled on her heel, flipped her hand at him, then walked faster.

"Hold up," he said. "I'll walk you through the park."

She gave him eyebrows. *Why?*

"Make sure you're all right."

"Ha. What you gonna do, protect me? Look at you." She had the nerve to smirk at his lanky, unmanly body. "You can't do nothing."

She was hitting him again. Stinging him. And like the night he charged down from his rooftop, he let her.

"I'd at least try."

Again her face said, *Why?*

There was nothing left to lose. In another fifteen minutes he would miss the bank's closing time. She was already disgusted with him. Nothing mattered.

"I can't stop thinking about you," he told her. "I wonder if you sleep at night or if you toss and turn."

She didn't react.

"I wonder if you went alone to be tested. If you was scared when you told the police."

She laughed, "Ha!" Big. Loud. From that laugh he knew she had done neither, and now he was disgusted with her.

"I don't understand you, girl."

"Ha, ha. What a big surprise."

"You go for Chinese herbs and to church, but you can't report it?"

"Why go to the police?" she said coolly, almost singing. "Did they come when I cry out? What can they do? Get back my stuff?"

He wanted to be mad at her, but she was right. Even he would run from the police before he'd run to them. But she should have done something, he thought.

"People should know," he said. "We could put up flyers."

"Flyers. Ha."

She was trying to make herself seem older, laughing at his innocence. It only made him angry.

"That's good," he said. "Laugh. Take herbs. Get on your knees. Pray."

"Leave me alone." She walked faster, but he easily matched her stride. He had not found her after all this time so he could fight with her.

"Look. I'm sorry, girl, I'm sorry," he said until she slowed her pace. Even so, she wouldn't look at him.

"I spoke out wrong," he said. "You've been through a lot. I want you to know, I'll go with you to get test—"

"They don't have nothing on me!" she said, swatting him away with her hand. "They don't have their dirt on me, their babies on me! Nothing."

"I'm not saying—"

She turned and stuck her finger in his chest. "I take care of my business. I cleanse my blood. I don't need no one telling me about test."

You can't be clean. I saw you.

He regretted thinking it, even for that second, for it was as if she could see the reflected image in his eyes of herself lying naked. She struck out at him with her fist, wild and off-balance, but he anticipated it and caught her balled hand before it made impact. She regained her footing and pushed him with both hands.

"You think I'm filth? I am disease? Then go! Get. Leave me. I don't need you. Leave me. Just leave me alone!" And she said more in Creole.

"I don't think that. I only meant . . ." And he gave up trying to explain what he himself didn't understand.

"Just leave me alone."

"I can't."

She pushed him.

There was never any peace around her. Instead he felt sick and brave at the same time, ready to jump into the unknown only to be hit.

"I'm walking you home."

"That's what I don't like. You don't ask. You just follow me."

"Can I ask you now?"

"Ask me what? I don't even know you. You're a stranger. A strange boy."

"Can I walk you through the park?"

"If I say no?"

"Then that's that. I'll stand right here while you go."

"And you won't follow me?"

He shook his head no.

"And you will stay out of my business?"

He nodded.

"Say it."

"I'll stay out of your business."

"And you will leave me alone?"

"You'll never see me again."

"You promise? Your word?"

"My word."

There. He lied to her. His most solemn word he gave

her, and he lied. It wasn't as hard a thing to do as he thought. He would always hope to find her and hope she would want to be found.

"My name is Thulani."

She said "Tulani," low enough so he could hear she did not pronounce the *h*. And they finished their walk in silence.

Once beyond the park and back in the world with everyone else, they watched out for cars and dodged people. The bankbook still in his pocket jabbed him. He knew he'd have to face Truman and Shakira when he put the undeposited money on the table. Their ranting would be endless, but it didn't matter. He was going to walk her, the girl, as long as she let him.

When they got to her house on Franklin Avenue, she said, "Now go," but he waited at the curb while she put the key in the door. As she opened the door and the window curtains parted, then closed from inside, she turned to him and said, "I am Ysa."

SEVEN

Every morning after he set his birds free, Thulani walked to the corner of Franklin and waited across the street from her house, hoping to catch Ysa on her way to school. His heart would say, Go to the buzzer, call out her name. After all, he told himself, they were hardly strangers. They had talked. They had argued. She had given him her name—something she wouldn't have done unless she intended him to use it. Even so, he couldn't bring himself to her door to press the buzzer. For a month he stood in the same spot from seven o'clock until eight, watching the window curtains part occasionally. Then he'd leave for school.

He didn't give up once inside school grounds. He took to roaming the halls of Erasmus Hall High, peering into classrooms from door windows on the chance that he would see her. He'd press his face against the glass and look for her hair, a mass of ringlets piled on her head, or even better, he'd seek out a rainbow among the rows of browns, blacks, and grays. Color would lead him to Ysa.

He roamed the halls during first and second periods and wondered how he could have missed her before. She could have been there all along, walking down Eastern Parkway as he stood above her on his roof. She could have been one of those who gave him "cut eyes" when he bumped into her in the hallways. He had been in a fog and hadn't seen what was in front of him. Since the time his mother died, no one existed. No one—except his birds—could touch him or be with him. Then there was Ysa. The girl whose scream pulled him from sleep, whose naked body wore his jersey. The girl who both rendered him speechless and drew him out. Out from his roof, out of his silence, out where he heard his own voice. Out of himself. All he wanted was to find her, touch her, talk to her, be in the world with her.

"Where your pass, son?"

Thulani released the doorknob and faced the hall patrol. He *could* run, but he had been caught. It didn't matter. "Don't have one."

He was promptly thrown into detention.

The next day he did it again. Peered into the windows of classes in session, hoping to find her. He observed hundreds of girls sitting in classrooms. Pretty girls wearing jeans and tops the colors of fall. Girls in curls and braids, short hair, ponytails, hair up, hair down. Girls writing in loose-leafs, passing notes, or staring at chalkboards. Some had even smiled at him, catching him off guard and making him feel good. But as pretty as they were, none of these girls was her.

He had only her name, Ysa, to go on and where she lived. He had no last name, although he was quite sure she was Haitian. He knew that she surrounded herself with color, believed in herbs, confession, and prayer, and that her little breasts would fit his mouth.

He also knew he couldn't continue like this, hanging outside her house or roaming the halls hoping to find her. He decided to seek out some Haitian girls and describe Ysa. As big as it was, the school had a decent representation of Haitian students. Surely someone knew her or attended mass with her at St. Augustine's. Haitian students stuck with one another the way Chinese stuck with Chinese, and Pakistanis stuck with Pakistanis. If he had to go up to every Haitian girl to find her class schedule, he would.

In his social studies class he spotted Janine

Desravines, a girl he remembered from elementary school and junior high. Janine had always been a fairly popular girl, always the center of her group. If anyone knew Ysa, she would.

He tried to get her attention at the end of social studies, but Janine and her friends were already out of the classroom. He followed them out to their lockers and called her by name, but she didn't respond. He knew she was messing with him, but he didn't care. He wasn't going away. Finally one of Janine's friends, a girl in brown, tapped her and pointed in his direction.

"There's this girl," he said quickly, because all eyes were on him. "Haitian girl. Lives with her mother or grandmother on Franklin. Wears a lot of colors."

Janine and the three other girls giggled. It was the kind of thing girls did well. Cut a man down to size. If he had to take their abuse to find his girl, he would. "Her name is Ysa. Do you know her? If she goes to Erasmus?"

Janine conferred with her group in Creole, tossing her name, Ysa, up and down in what he felt were derisive tones.

"You sure she's not Jamaican?" Janine asked.

They all giggled.

"She's Haitian."

Janine shot back something, and she and her friends burst out laughing.

He started to walk away.

Janine called after him, "No. We don't know your Ysa."

Later in the cafeteria Janine sat next to him while he drank milk and said, "You know Julie?"

"Julie?"

She gestured to the girl in the brown top.

"She thinks you're okay."

He blushed, then smiled, not expecting this at all. That someone would think he was cute.

"While you're looking for this Ysa, you should think about it."

Janine rejoined her group. They began talking excitedly and giving him face, particularly the girl in brown, Julie. They wouldn't leave him alone until he smiled back.

He did not go first to the roof as he usually did when he got home. Instead he flew upstairs to the bathroom, locked the door, and stood before the mirror to see what he had. To see why Julie smiled at him and told her girlfriends she thought he was okay and why Janine was bold enough to tell him so.

In the mirror he saw his mother's slanted eyes. Her long lashes. Her lips as he remembered them, well defined and full. Not so much from memory, but from the photo in his bedroom, he saw his father's prominent features, his strong nose and jawline, red-brown complexion smoothed over high cheekbones.

He smiled at his endowments. He had looks a girl could find attractive.

Since the age of thirteen up until nearly sixteen, his face had been eclipsed by hooded sweatshirts. Even through hot summers he wore hoods. He would have worn them the past summer if not for a police sketch of a mugger that appeared on the news. The robber, a black male between the ages of sixteen and twenty, was armed and considered dangerous. He vaguely fitted Thulani's height and build and committed his crimes wearing hooded sweatshirts. Before the broadcast was over, Shakira had broken through his door, gathered up every hooded sweatshirt he owned, and stuffed them into a Hefty bag, which she set out with the trash. "They round you up first, ask questions later."

If he wasn't so angry at Shakira, he might even have laughed.

There was a knock on the bathroom door. "Thulani. I have to get in there."

"I'll be out."

"You've been in there an hour. Let me in."

She exaggerated. He'd been in there five, ten minutes.

When he finally opened the door, she pushed him out and closed the door to pee. With her belly even larger she was always in the bathroom.

He went downstairs to wait for her. Today he decided to give her what she always wanted: in. He was going to talk to her. Ask for her opinion.

Shakira had changed clothes and appeared to be a little flushed, but Thulani let these things slip his notice.

"Suppose you like a girl," he began, though Shakira seemed preoccupied, putting away her still warm but unserved dinner. "But she's kinda hard, uh, hard to know. Then there's this new girl."

Even preoccupied, Shakira wouldn't spoil this opportunity. He'd never give her another chance.

"First Girl givin' ya hard time?"

He nodded.

"Ya sure New Girl like you?"

"Yeh."

"Ya like New Girl?"

"She cute."

"Which one on your mind?"

"First Girl."

"Then stop triflin' with New Girl and call Truman."

"Truman?"

"What, I stuttah? Call him. Tell him to get to the hospital quick. Then call the EMS."

"Hospital?"

"I tried to wait, but I can't go no longer."

Thulani did not do things in the order that Shakira had asked. First he ran up to the roof to leave the cage open for his birds. Then he called 911 for the EMS. They asked him questions about the contractions, blood, and water—questions he couldn't answer. They said they would be there in fifteen minutes. Then he called the dispatcher's office at the subway station to leave the message for Truman.

The EMS ambulance came in thirty minutes. They took Shakira's pulse and put a stethoscope on her belly. Thulani wanted no part of it when the female driver raised up her skirt. He waited outside until Shakira came out on a stretcher. The EMS driver said the baby was not crowning but they should get to the hospital quick.

Thulani locked up the house and rode in the ambulance with his sister-in-law. Every five minutes she dug her nails into his arm. He was relieved when they arrived at the hospital and Shakira was wheeled away, glad when Truman finally arrived.

Two hours later he was an uncle and Truman was a father. When Truman emerged from the delivery room, his stone face broke and tears gushed. Thulani had never seen his brother cry, not even during the time that

Mommy went away. Died. Truman said the baby girl was healthy, she looked like Shakira, and they would name her Eula after Mommy. He gave praises to Jah, then told Thulani, "There is but one child in our house. You have to help out. Get a job."

EIGHT

For three days Thulani knew the peace of a quiet home. Everything was as his mother intended, with both sons caring for her home. Thulani cooked and did laundry while Truman painted Eula's room. Once the baby was brought home, Shakira's family would visit often, so the house had to be ready.

During this time Truman never repeated what he had said in the hospital or asked his brother how the job hunt was going. This was not Truman's way. He stated himself plainly and once. Even though he ate Thulani's oxtails, wore the shirts that Thulani washed and ironed, and likened all of Thulani's housework to their mother's, it was understood that Thulani was to seek work.

On the morning that Shakira and Eula were to

come home, Truman said, "I've been thinking." This meant that he and Shakira had been discussing this new thought in detail and it was now time to bring it to light.

Thulani waited for the other shoe to drop, and at that moment he fully comprehended the expression. In Truman's pause he tried to match the tone of Truman's last word with the many possibilities that could follow. He thought of the many things Truman and Shakira could devise and held his breath.

"You show no inclination for school," Truman began.

He could breathe freely. This was true. He spent more time roaming the hallways looking for Ysa than sitting in class taking notes and fretting over the SATs.

"Mommy left you some money for college."

"Yeh, so?"

"The money will be better spent toward a down payment on a house in Jersey."

"What? Leave Brooklyn?"

"A child canna grow on concrete. We need a house with a yard."

"They have homes with yards in Brooklyn," Thulani said.

"We're leaving Brooklyn," Truman told him.

"The brownstone's worth money. Mommy always said—"

"It needs too much work, Thulani. Who's going to

do it? I'm selling the brownstone. In two years we're gone. End of discussion."

Is this what Truman and Shakira did at night? Thought of ways to choke him with their plans? Steal Mommy from his memory? Kill off his birds?

Truman put his plate in the sink for Thulani to wash. He said, "You'll be eighteen before long. Old enough to be responsible with the money Mommy left. That money plus my share will make the down payment until we sell the brownstone."

The other shoe landed. There was nothing left to say.

Thulani ran up to his roof to unlatch the dovecote. Even though he had no morning treats, no cereal or seeds, his birds still gathered at his feet and perched on his arms and shoulders. Bruno landed on his head. He needed to surround himself with their cooing, their feathers.

Leave Mommy's house? Leave his birds? Leave Brooklyn? And leave Ysa—if he ever found her again. He couldn't leave yet.

He took Yoli to his heart and stroked her breast feathers. When she grew restless in his grip, and Bruno became jealous, Thulani let her go. He let them all go.

Shakira and Eula were home by the time he came in from school. He wanted to get a good look at his niece, although it was impossible. Shakira did not let her child out of her arms. Even when her own mother, sisters, aunts, and cousins warned her Eula would be spoiled, Shakira never turned her eyes from her daughter.

With much reluctance Shakira brought Eula to the nursery and placed her in her bassinet. While Shakira was being catered to by her family, Thulani saw his opportunity. He had seen the baby but wanted to have this moment alone with her.

"Look at you," he whispered. "Just look at you." Truman was right. She was the very picture of Shakira but with Truman's eyes. Before Thulani could reach down into the bassinet to hold her, the door flew open.

"*Cha!* Ya crazy or what? She's had no shots and you smellin' like pigeon shit. Gwan from her!"

For five days Thulani cleaned, cooked, and did homework while Shakira rested and fussed with her baby. Once Shakira was ready to resume housework, Thulani went back to his rooftop or went looking for Ysa at the Chinese herb store, St. Augustine's, or the park. When he thought of it, he approached storeowners in his neighborhood for after-school jobs. Although these inquiries for work were halfhearted on his part, he knew he could not continue to live off his brother's earnings. With the addition of Eula to the family, his life changed. He was suddenly a man, expected to give up everything he knew simply because he had no plans of his own.

In class he drifted in and out of the finer points of bacteria and trinomials. He flirted with Julie but dreamed of Ysa. Nothing held his interest longer than fifteen minutes. School was simply the sitting place. Sitting and longing. Longing to be elsewhere, and having nowhere in mind.

He would do enough work to be promoted, then graduate the following year. If he couldn't keep himself in school, he would take the GED exam. He might have tried college for a year to please his mother, but she was gone, and he couldn't envision a lecture hall as a place to be, only as a place to sit.

For now he needed a part-time job. Any job would do. Just something to put money on the table once a week for his share of the groceries. If he didn't find a part-time job on his own, Truman and Shakira would find work for him.

He took the bus downtown to scout out possible employers. Most fast-food places welcomed him, but he did not crave hamburgers, and he would be knee-deep in burgers. He thought about the big library at Grand Army Plaza, but this would keep him indoors. He needed to be outside. Perhaps get work as a messenger. That would take him around town without a boss to like for her and why he didn't care with Julie. And now, as she urged him, her face willing and fearful, he removed his clothes. He said, "If you want to, you have to do it."

He lay on his back with his knees up. "I'm here," he said. "But you have to do it."

"Don't move . . . ," she said.

"I won't."

". . . until I'm ready."

She lifted her leg over his hips and knelt over him.

"Just be still," she said. "Stay."

"We don't have t—"

"Shh, shh. Stay. I come down slow."

"I'm here," he said. "I'm here."

She began to descend, her hands reaching for his. As she made her way down, half an inch at a time, it was all he could do not to move. He was flooded with her and the colors she carried in her. Now in him.

When she met him fully, he watched her eyes open and close in what he knew was pain, and what he prayed was the flush of vibrant colors. Behind her hung a sea of indigo and one hundred gold and turquoise eyes that would not blink.

EIGHTEEN

"Are you all right?"

They had been sitting on their park bench waiting until the sun went down, which was when he
usually brought her home.

She laughed at him. "You asked me that yester-
day, the day before, and the day before that."

He still worried. He could not help thinking he
had brought back the pain inflicted on her almost a
year ago in the alley. While she smiled and assured
him otherwise, he could not believe her completely.
Even so, he also knew he would not undo any of it.
If he never felt another thing in his life, he had felt
Ysa, and that was not to be taken back.

He said, "I have to make sure you're all right.
You're my girl."

"For now, Tulani," she said, her eyes shining bright under the park lights, her smile faint. "For now, while we're sitting on our bench. But I'm my girl. I have to be all right, for me."

He almost spoke, but the voice, his mother's voice, told him to be still. To be satisfied that she let him sit close to her. Hold her hand. Like Ysa said, for now.

"Okay." He gave in. "Then kiss me here"—he pointed to his lips—"and here"—to one eyelid—"here"—the other eyelid—"then we'll go."

Then he kissed her as she did him but resisted the urge to give her one last squeeze before they started toward her house. He took her hand and remembered what she once asked of him: to let go when it was time to let go.

Thulani came in quietly and lifted the lids on pots on the stove to see what Shakira had cooked for supper. He made himself a small plate of oxtails and vegetables and sat down to eat. He chewed around the bone and said to himself, I'll show her Mommy's recipe before they go.

Thinking of the move only reminded him he had no plan. The contentment he felt from being with Ysa faded.

"Good, you're here," Shakira said. Her voice was excited.

Truman followed behind her. From his expression, the exasperation of having been cut off in mid-speech, Thulani knew they had been arguing.

"Here he sits," Truman said. Thulani filled in the rest, which was "eating my food."

"Eat!" Shakira ordered Thulani. "Eat everything. There is more in the refrigerator."

"What did I walk into?" Thulani asked.

"I'll tell you, braa," Shakira said. "Eula and I are not going to Jersey. We're going to Lincoln Place." Lincoln Place was where her parents lived.

Thulani put his fork down.

"Eat! It is *our* food. Not his," she said, pointing to Truman, "not mine, not yours. Our food. Eat well, because I'm packing up me and Eula to go home."

"Shakira, stop your drama. You're my wife, and my wife and daughter comes with me."

Shakira said, "Give Thulani his money. Then your wife and your daughter come with you."

"You're messing with tings not your business," Truman warned, but Shakira did not seem to care or change her stance.

"Not my business? What? Truman d'na marry *I and I*. Truman marry Shakira. True?"

Thulani nodded. True.

"One flesh, one blood, true?" she asked her husband.

"*Cha!* How can I sit in my house and enjoy my washing machine, my flower garden, when I know Thulani roam the streets with no home? You think that makes me happy? You think I can have peace? Raise my daughter to be decent when we steal from her uncle?"

"Thulani has a place with us. This is how I planned it."

"But this is not what Madda Eula wanted. I sat with her, Truman. These are not her wishes, and I'm not a thief. I canna *live* in a house not mine."

Truman turned to Thulani. "You see you cause? I try to keep the family together, you split everyone t'hell apart."

When he came home the next evening, Thulani found a bankbook on the table. It was in both his and his mother's names. He opened it. The deposits had begun the year he was three and ended the year he was thirteen. The interest had added up through the years. He closed the bankbook and put it in his wallet.

"You have to make your way on that, Thulani," Shakira said. "And y'beddanot make me out a fool. Y'hear me?"

He hugged his sister-in-law and promised he wouldn't disappoint her. By the same token, as he hugged her, a world of things occurred to him, now that he had means.

NINETEEN

"I will be gone a month," he told Mr. Moon.

"No job when you come back," Mr. Moon replied.

"How can you be like that, Mr. Moon? I have to see my father in Jamaica."

"No come, no job."

In spite of the finality in Mr. Moon's tone, Thulani was not worried. He could get his job back if he had to. It just wouldn't be easy.

He lifted his newly repaired camera to take a picture of Mr. Moon. As usual Mr. Moon quickly put his hands up.

Ysa, on the other hand, posed for many pictures in her graduation dress, which she had designed herself. She had chosen a bright white fabric that picked up colors when hit by the sunlight. Iridescent, she called it.

He took pictures of her in her cap and gown standing with a camera-shy Tant Rosie. He managed to get one close-up of her face at the moment that her hand touched the fake diploma.

Ysa was anxious to have photographs taken of the dress. Once the ceremony was over, she removed her blue robe and cap and gave them to Tant Rosie to bring home, while she and Thulani went to the park. There Thulani tried to capture Ysa in her dress as the sun set off its many colors.

He promised to bring her copies of the photos when he returned from his trip.

"No, no. Mail them to me," she insisted. "I want to look forward to receiving them."

"I'll be back soon," he promised, but she did not seem satisfied. Her eyes were sad. She said, "I wish we could stay here in the park."

He kissed her on her lips and on her closed eyelids as she had always done for him. "I'll be back soon," he said.

They sat on their bench. She said, "Tulani, I want to tell you something, but I don't want you to be upset."

What?

"I felt pain."

"Ysa." He squeezed her hands, but she pulled back.

"No, no. Not how you think. I mean, I felt pain, but you didn't hurt me. Do you see the difference?"

"Not really."

He took her hands again, gently. She said, "Think about it while you're flying far away in your big tin bird. It will come to you. You'll understand. Then think about me and our little time together."

He tried to laugh at her, but she was serious. "I'll be back before you miss me," he promised. "I just need to see my father. You'll see."

"Tulani, that's what you say. But you will see the place you were born. Your father. How rich the land. You'll be home. I know."

"I'll be back before—"

"Ssh, ssh," she said. "Let's sit here and not speak." After a while she said, "You can sing me my lullaby." And he did.

Shakira gave Thulani the addresses of her relatives and directions to his father's house. Eula gave her uncle a drooly kiss. Truman had already given him the bankbook, and that was all that he would give.

Truman and Shakira had already begun packing for their new home. Thulani wanted to leave before the house was stripped of everything his mother put in it. He did not want to be there when they left. He had to be the first to go.

He packed neatly. His clothes and possessions all

went into one large duffel bag. He would carry the box of photographs and the camera with him on the plane.

He looked back at his bed, the dresser, the night-stand, and finally the walls. He had to let go of everything. Everything except the skirt, which he saved for last to pack. He removed each nail carefully so as not to tear the fabric. This took some care, as he had driven the nails deep into the wall. The silklike fabric fell into his arms with ease when he released the last nail. He laid Ysa's skirt out on his bed and folded it in half, fourths, then eighths, turning the gold and turquoise on the wrong side. Even so, he could still see her eyes before him, opening and closing, opening and closing, opening and closing. . . .

Read on for a sneak peek at Rita Williams-Garcia's

A SITTING IN ST. JAMES

I

Patience. Even as time leaps three score and seven years, all that lies between that time and now will be made known. Patience.
July 1860

"THISBE," MADAME SAID TO THE DARK-SKINNED GIRL standing to her right. "Go out to the gallery. Tell me what he is doing." Her French was clipped, but notes of wicked humor peppered the command. Madame Sylvie didn't speak the more relaxed Louisiana French or French Creole. Having lived nearly sixty of her eighty years in St. James, Louisiana, she still only spoke the French of her childhood spent in her family vineyard and in Queen Marie Antoinette's Petit Trianon and in her country hamlet. Madame did not consider herself Creole, and this was true—Madame and her husband were French born. Her son, Lucien, however, like white Catholics born to French or Spanish parents on Louisiana soil, proclaimed himself a proud Creole, much to Madame's objections and disdain. For how could her son be what Black Creoles also called themselves?

"Yes, Madame," the girl answered. She left Madame's salon through the opened shutter doors and stepped outside onto the wood-planked gallery. The gallery faced the river but didn't wrap around the two-story house. She couldn't see her family's cabin in the quarter, or the rows of green cane stalks stretching without end behind the house. Her clearest views were front-facing, of the river, the live oaks that lined the path and served as a walkway, the garden, the far-off man-made pond, and the garçonnière where Madame's grandson, Byron, stayed. To see the cement monument to Bayard Guilbert, the site that Madame's son, Lucien Guilbert, had last night threatened to take action, Thisbe went to the upriver end of the gallery and leaned, holding on to the railing with one hand. The wide-hipped roof gave her plenty of shade, but she cupped her other hand above her brow to tamp down the sheer might of the July sun that cursed and blessed the small plantation. She saw enough to report to Madame: Monsieur Lucien sitting on his white horse, overseeing the work at hand. Four Black men, men he had earlier claimed he couldn't spare from the cane fields, digging at the obelisk that bore his father's name. Thisbe hoped one of the four men was her father, but she could see he wasn't among them. It had been months since she had visited with her family, although they were housed in the quarter, not more than five hundred feet behind the big house, or Le Petit Cottage. Still, it was a comforting thought to imagine her father being close enough to wave to her, although she dared not wave back while she served Madame Sylvie.

Twenty seconds hadn't yet passed, but Thisbe, aware her Madame wasn't a patient woman, returned to the salon to report back.

"And?"

"Monsieur Lucien watches the men dig Monsieur Bayard's stone, Madame Sylvie." These words, eleven in total, were the longest utterance the girl would speak in Madame's presence that day. That being the case, she purposely extended each sound before she returned to a vault of relative silence. Still, she hoped for more opportunities to speak. French, Louisiana French Creole, English, pidgin English. It didn't matter. Perhaps Madame would ask which men and if they found anything.

"Digging!" Madame Sylvie threw her head back and laughed, each cackle catching in her throat and mouth, a sound like dishes breaking. "So close, my son. So close!"

Thisbe bent to aid Madame, but the much older woman waved her off and lifted herself up under her own power, gripping the arm of her favorite perch, a faded rose brocade throne with a curved mahogany frame and legs. The little throne was a gift from her husband. A joke and reminder of her former surroundings at Le Petit Trianon. After her years of service as plantation mistress, Sylvie wanted nothing more than to sit on this little chair and to be served. Madame Sylvie, the *maîtresse*, was petite at eighty, but not frail. Still, in spite of being waved away, Thisbe remained close and helped her mistress out onto the gallery.

3

"And Beee-rohn?" Madame's tongue turned her grandson's name, Byron, after the English poet, into a French confection. "Do you see him? Does he stand at the big tree and wait?"

Thisbe peered toward the grand live oak, the centerpiece of Le Petit Cottage. She and Madame knew the grandson's routine since he had returned home from West Point. Lately, it was to close the commissary at noon, walk to the live oak, and then stand like a guardsman with his hands behind his back for as long as an hour. Sometimes ninety minutes. There were so few customers to buy goods at the commissary. Who had cash? After his hour or so of standing, Byron would then walk back to the commissary in no hurry.

"My fan!" Madame said.

Thisbe was light on her feet in her shiny black leather ankle boots. Her skirt barely rustled when she pirouetted and disappeared into the salon. She was quick about retrieving the ivory-handled fan and rushed to the gallery to give the fan to Madame.

Was he guarding the plantation? This didn't seem likely. But why stand there? Madame and servant looked toward the big tree and waited for something about the routine to change.

Byron's first two years at West Point straightened his spine and opened his chest. He knew his grandmother sat out on the gallery watching, which was precisely why he kept his back to the house, even though she couldn't see his expression. These were private, pleasurable moments for him. Who would want to be

4

spied upon from afar and then picked apart later in the dining room? With his back turned, he was to himself. With his face lifted, eyes closed, the kiss of a breeze rising off the Mississippi swirled around his nape and ears and was gone. A memory. A smile. And now longing. Indescribable longing. And waiting.

For all practical purposes, Byron was an engaged man. The negotiations had been made between his father and Colonel Duhon, the father of Eugénie Duhon. The wedding would take place two years from this past June—five days following Byron's graduation from West Point. He and Eugénie had met three times, but mainly wrote letters. There were no mothers—both having died shortly after childbirth—to press for a shorter and more involved engagement. The two young people, however—Byron, soon to be twenty, and Eugénie, seventeen—were agreeable to the discreet and extended family arrangement, with a proper announcement forthcoming at the right time.

In every way, Byron was a dutiful son. Most important, he was the Guilbert legal heir. (Rosalie, his quadroon half sister, and any other half siblings that had been farmed to other plantations or sold to settle debt had no legal claim to the plantation.) It was Byron Guilbert whose steps in life mattered. In spite of his innermost conflicts, Byron would do what was expected of him. He would marry Eugénie Duhon and assume the management of Le Petit Cottage so his father could drink bourbon, gamble at racetracks, and read the old poets. Byron would produce heirs, preferably two, as neither his father nor grandfather had much luck in producing white heirs. In time, he would hand off the plantation to the next legal son, or daughter's husband if it came to that. He found the idea of producing legal heirs amusing. A legal heir, maybe two, would be all that he could muster, as he didn't share his father's or grandfather's lust for Black women, or for women of any color, for that matter.

To refuse or escape his life didn't occur to him. Neither of these choices was an option. But this moment, this reverie of stirred air and memory, made the impossibility he harbored within that much sweeter.